# MEENA'S STORY

## *FLIGHT TO FREEDOM*

## A True Story

*by*

**SWAPNA GUPTA**

MEENA'S STORY: Flight to Freedom



Publication: October 2020

Published in Canada by
Bayeux Arts, Inc.
2403, 510 – 6th Avenue, S.E.
Calgary, Canada T2G 1L7

www.bayeux.com



Cover Design: Lumina Datamatics

Book design by Lumina Datamatics



Library and Archives Canada Cataloguing in Publication

Title: Meena's story : flight to freedom / Swapna Gupta.

Names: Gupta, Swapna, 1941- author.

Identifiers: Canadiana (print) 20200286625 | Canadiana (ebook) 20200286676 | ISBN 9781988440507 (hardcover) | ISBN 9781988440514 (EPUB)

Classification: LCC PS8613.U688 M44 2020 | DDC C813/.6—dc23

The ongoing publishing activities of Bayeux Arts Digital — Traditional Publishing under its varied imprints are supported by the Government of Alberta, Alberta Multimedia Development Fund, and the Government of Canada through the Book Publishing Industry Development Program.

Patrimoine canadien   Canadian Heritage

Printed in Canada

# MEENA'S STORY

# Chapter 1

It's only ten o' clock in the morning. The sun is scorching hot already. The air is still, with not even a slight breeze to breathe ripples across the golden wheat fields ready for harvest. Grey smoke rises in the distance as farmers burn down swaths of wheat stubble. There hangs a sense of foreboding in the air. Ali is pensive as he looks out of the latticed verandah of his home. It was only recently that an aunt in Hyderabad had found his family this house in Malir on the outskirts of Karachi.

Ali feels deeply troubled. The last few months have been very difficult for him, his young English wife, two sons and two daughters. They had left their family home in Hyderabad to begin a new life in Pakistan. Little did Ali know that he, a Muslim, would face such intense hostility in this new country. Only a fortnight ago, in the middle of the night, they had to run for their lives and hide in the fields for hours after the old caretaker of the house had been beaten up and threatened with more. "How dare you let the house to be rented by those Mahajirs?"

If only Ali had understood earlier the intense hatred Pakistanis of Sindhi descent harbored against him, he might have thought twice about moving to Karachi. To the people of Sindh, he was unwanted because he was an immigrant, a Mahajir. But where would he have gone? He had lived in pre-partition India and also England, but he wanted to serve Pakistan and help it grow into a strong nation. The communal tensions he saw upon coming to Karachi shocked him. It seemed the Punjabi Muslims of Sindh detested Muslim Mahajirs like him. Before long, the hatred had boiled over into the 1948 Karachi riots.

As he looked out of his verandah, Ali recalled the parts of Karachi scarred by the riots, horrific tales of murder and mayhem, that filled his heart with fear. The riots were intended to drive Hindu Sindhis out of Pakistan, but soon engulfed Mahajirs as well.

Ali looked around the verandah, and stopped to stare at the faded calendar hanging on the wall. The sun beat relentlessly on it, discoloring the paper. When the wind blew the calendar swayed from side to side, the metal headband scratching rhythmically against the wall, scratching a permanent semi-circle. Yes, it was the beginning of *Ramadan.*

Although liked by his peers in the office where he worked for the Karachi Transportation, there were many who were increasingly envious of Ali's quick promotions. And many who of course resented him being a Mahajir.

The Sindh government had set up a Peace Board made up of Hindu and Muslim members to maintain order in the troubled province. P.V. Tahilramani, a Hindu, was secretary of the Peace Board. Karachi newspapers had carried details of the riots, and how Tahilramani rushed to the office of the Sindh Chief Minister, Khuhro, to inform the chief minister that the Sikhs in Guru Mandir areas of Karachi were being killed. According to Khuhro, senior bureaucrats and police officials were nowhere to be found and he rushed to the scene at around 12.30 p.m. where he saw "mobs of refugees armed with knives and sticks storming the temples". Khuhro tried to stem the violence. Mr. Jinnah, the Founder of Pakistan, was pleased with his efforts. But death still took a terrible toll.

Because the house was large and isolated, inhabited by only a young couple and four young children in this remote desert-like landscape, danger lurked in every corner. Their scattered neighbors were nomadic tribals from the neighboring state of Baluchistan. Many of them were known to snatch babies, or so it was believed. They also raised armadillos and intentionally sent them into nearby houses to torment and bite the residents. Another common belief. After the attack on the caretaker who lived at the rear of the house, Ali had started to sleep with a gun.

It is not as if there weren't other houses nearby. Most notably, a retreat of the Amir of Bahawalpur, Nawab Sadiq Mohammad Khan Abbasi V, a friend of Mr. Jinnah's. The Nawabs were friends and allies of the British, until the British hurriedly dumped them all like unwanted mistresses when the Empire collapsed with India's independence and Pakistan's emergence. Even Ali, with his British wife, couldn't say they were the Amir's neighbors.

Eight month's later, Mr. Jinnah was dead. His dream was that of a secular Pakistan. Religion never mattered in his public or private life. Disagreeing with Gandhi's mixture of politics with religion, Jinnah left the Indian Congress Party. Gandhi used the Khilafat (rule of the *khalifa*), a religious issue, to unite the Hindus and Muslims in India. Jinnah opposed it both in the Muslim League and Congress even at the risk of his political career. Kamal Pasha, who had abolished the *Khilafat* and introduced democracy and modernism in Turkey, became his role model. That's what Mr. Jinnah was building his vision of Pakistan on.

Living in Hyderabad, Ali had been privy to the unfolding drama of independence, and experienced both joy and heartbreak. In particular, he remembered a remark Jinnah had shared with an Indian politician friend, "You destroy your *Pandit* and we will destroy our *Mullah* and there will be communal peace."

July 8, 1950. It was indeed the beginning of *Ramadan.* Still staring into the distance from the verandah, Ali is startled by his wife Zarina placing her hand gently on his arm to summon him to see the children finish their breakfast before heading for school.

"It is a very beautiful land, is it not?" Ali asks Zarina. They have both been up since early morning and Ali confesses to being a bit weary, having had a restless night and not much sleep. But he shifts his gaze again to the landscape and gradually his face softens, and the tired lines on his brow start to melt away.

Somewhere in the distant landscape there lay the beginnings of the Indus civilization. Ali had vowed to take the family to see the site of the excavations in Mohenjodaro which had begun as late as the 1920s, even though the British had established the East India Company on the sub-continent as early as 1600. In the desert sand in front of his eyes, Ali thought he could see the British army – horses, camels, and foot soldiers – marching across a largely ignored territory towards Afghanistan in 1842 to establish a friendly ruler on the throne as a bulwark against Russian territorial ambitions in the region. But the expedition ended in an ignominious defeat with the British army decimated as they retreated from Kabul.

Zarina knew this history well, having been encouraged by Ali to explore the collection on Sindh in Hyderabad's magnificent Asafia Library before coming to Pakistan. She visited the library often, not only looking for books but also looking out of the windows in wonder at all the life passing by along the River Musi on whose bank the library was built in 1891 with help from the Nizam of Hyderabad's chief engineer, Nawab Khan Bahadur Mirza Akbar Baig.

At night, before they fell asleep, Zarina would recount to Ali all her day's readings, often to the surprise of Ali who was unaware of much of his own city's history, let alone the history of Sindh. They had many a laugh over the Nizam's engineer's endless name.

It was Zarina who had told him of the British debacle in 1842 and how the event turned the focus on Sindh. Not only did it then assume greater importance as a defence against external aggression, but its subjugation was required to redeem national pride. So, General Charles Napier was brought in to establish a permanent British presence. Crushing all opposition, he achieved his objective at the battle of Milani in February 1843, followed by annexation the next month. For the next four years, General Napier remained in Sindh as Governor with the army in charge.

Ali's thoughts returned to Mohenjodaro. "All we need to do is drive north to Larkana which will take us to the ruins. They are three or four thousand years old, and the drive shouldn't take us longer than six hours," he said.

"Doesn't Mohenjodaro mean 'Mound of the Dead?" asked Zarina.

"Yes, I believe it does, although it doesn't make sense to me. Because life flowed out of Mohenjodaro and populated the entire Indian subcontinent."

"From what I've seen in books," said Zarina, "the Indus Civilization was quite magnificent with craftsmen showing an amazing mastery of carving stone and modelling clay."

"Yes," added Ali, "and there were Buddhist *stupas* and Shiva temples. Don't know if they were at each others' throats as we are today."

"Some day, we must also go and see more recent wonders of Islamic architecture too, shouldn't we?" asked Zarina.

"Yes, of course," agreed Ali. "After all, it was in Sindh that Islam established its first foothold on the subcontinent. Sindh was the name for the western half of the land of al-Hind-wa-l-Sindh, the mighty bloc radiating to the east and west from the banks of the Indus river. It was the stuff of legends since the days of Alexander the Great." Ali looked thoughtful. He added, "I should not look back at my days in Hyderabad and imagine we made a mistake in coming to Pakistan." He paused.

Zarina gently squeezed his fingers and said, "Of course not. This is where we will build our future."

"It is almost as if I have come home," said Ali wistfully.

Zarina sighed and turned round slowly to face the day that lay ahead. They had been up since before dawn. Because of *Ramadan*, they prepare for their morning meal as they will not eat again until the sun goes down. This is very important to Ali and, although Zarina grew up in a Christian home in England, since her marriage to Ali she has happily chosen to follow the Shia Muslim customs.

But the children must have breakfast. They are too young to observe the fast of *Ramadan*. So Zarina wakes them up, Didu, Meena and Danny, to get them ready for school. She calls them to the breakfast table and serves them toast, milk and eggs. Little Tayab is too young for school and he wriggles out of his baby chair and hangs on to his mother's *chunni* (scarf). By the time the other children have had their breakfasts and got their school things together it is already mid morning and the sun is getting hotter.

Tayab was still hanging onto his mother. He is not going to school. His sister Meena couldn't help teasing him, "Why don't you come to school with us, Tayab?" Tayab clutched his mother even more tightly.

They waited for a neighbor's son, Ahmad, to come. He was in Meena's class and was a regular passenger in their car. Zarina asked Ahmad how his parents were doing this morning. "They are fine," replied Ahmad.

Ahmad and two of Zarina and Ali's children, Didu and Danny, piled into the back seat of the car. Meena sat in front between Ali who decided to drive, and the regular driver, Sher Khan. They waved back to Zarina who stood on the verandah with little Tayab. The dust raised by the car as it swung out of the gate forced her to quickly get back into the house with Tayab.

In the fields along the road to Karachi City, men were already at work, white turbans covering their heads against the relentless sun. "Why does Tayab stay at home," asked Danny suddenly, "and we have to go to school?"

"Because Tayab is a baby," Meena offered as an explanation.

"Also, because if you don't go to school, said Ali, pointing to the farm workers outside the window, "you might someday have to work like those men there. Would you like that?"

Didu wanted to throw something into the discussion. She looked wide-eyed at Ahmad sitting beside her and said, "In Hyderabad, two teachers came to the house to teach us." Ahmad looked duly impressed but questioned how they might play soccer with the boys if they didn't go to school. That seemed to end the discussion.

Danny became silent. Nobody else ventured an answer. After a while Sher Khan cleared his throat and said, "I never went to school, so I never worked in an office or in a school. I ended up driving other peoples' cars."

"But you are a very good driver, Sher Khan," Ali quickly pointed out. "And we're very happy when you drive us around the city, aren't we, children?"

"Yes, yes," everybody joined in. Sher Khan smiled broadly but said nothing.

They hit a long stretch of deserted road rolling over gentle hills and occasional curves. There wasn't much traffic. A car came and passed them from the opposite direction, raising a cloud of dust which engulfed the car. Ali swore softly under his breath.

The dust cleared ever so slowly. Before long another dust storm seemed to be gathering in the distance. The road ahead was now straight but gradual slope, bounded by brown, caked earth and sand. Gradually, a black speck appeared to take shape in the swirling dust advancing rapidly towards the car.

The distant speck was closing in fast, becoming larger and larger until it became a monstrous truck heading straight towards the car. Ali tried to swerve to the left, away from the approaching truck. But he was too late. The thunderous sound of the collision shattered the silence of the desert with the screeching of wheels, steam radiating from the crushed radiator, and the sudden flapping of wings as a startled flock of vultures feeding nearby on an animal carcass took flight.

Meena, in the front seat between her father Ali and Sher Khan has a vivid memory of the moments leading up to the crash. Larger. LARGER. **LARGER**. What she remembers next is her mother's face in the Karachi hospital where she had been taken, bleeding profusely from her injuries. Her sister Didu remained terrified for days and years as she remembered the lorry driver walking up to the car and threatening her, "You will not tell anyone what you saw. If you do, you will never live another day." For days, Danny, relatively unscathed like Didu, seemed to have lost his speech and his memory.

Ali, badly mangled and unconscious, was also moved to the Karachi General Hospital. Little Ahmad and Sher Khan had died on the spot.

## Chapter 2

Elizabeth Burdett has been in Hyderabad for a few days. She is full of memories of her recent voyage from Southampton and also feelings of trepidation over her impending meeting with her in-laws. Her husband Ali whom she married in England shortly before leaving the country has not told his mother about her. So, in a sense, she was not supposed to be here in India at all.

Considering the situation faced by Elizabeth and one of her friends, Catherine, one would be forgiven for imagining that London was facing an epidemic of young women falling in love with dashing Hyderabadi men. Catherine too faced a similar predicament because she wanted to marry one of Ali's friends, Akbar, who, like Ali, had recently left London for India.

Akbar had left London unmarried, but Elizabeth and Ali were far too gone in love. They went ahead with a civil marriage ceremony in London. Ali proposed to go ahead to Hyderabad and prepare his mother for Elizabeth to join him, and so he did. But Elizabeth grew impatient. When Catherine confided to her that she was planning to go to India to be with Akbar, the two young women made up their minds to travel together. Ali received word of their plans in a telegram. While secretly elated, Ali suggested the two women wait a little longer. He consulted with Akbar and found that he was even more unprepared.

The die is cast. The two women embark on their voyage on the Lloyd Triestino liner, *Conte Biancamano*, in March 1939. Europe was in turmoil, but the sounds of war in Europe had not yet crashed into Britain's consciousness. When the ship embarked in Genoa, the two women were astonished to see new passengers boarding their ship. They looked frightened, tired, and the children clung desperately to their mothers. There seemed little excitement in their faces about the voyage.

Soon, they would find out that the passengers who boarded the ship in Genoa were headed for an uncertain future and a refuge in Shanghai. They were escaping the Nazi rampage shaking the very foundations of European society.

The Jewish refugees on board were in sharp contrast to another small group of quiet and composed men who stayed together and, if asked by other passengers, often spoke about mountains, their beauty, their intoxicating challenges, and human frailty. These were members of the American Karakoram Expedition to K2, led by the famous climber, Fritz Wiessner. Elizabeth and Catherine admired these brave men from a distance. They knew from news reports that, a year earlier, Wiessner had already done a reconnaissance of K2, one of the most difficult mountains in the world.

And so the two women had crossed the ocean to be with the two men they had met in England and fallen in love with. It was also an expedition of sorts. When they first arrived, Ali suggested that they stay in the servant's quarters, unnoticed in the rest of their rambling house. Meanwhile, he would gently prepare his mother.

Elizabeth feels lonely and nervous as she waits for a fateful meeting. The past was like a dream gently stirring in her mind. She remembers the first time she met Ali. Elizabeth was getting off an escalator in London when it suddenly stopped and she was about to fall but, instead, she fell into the arms of a dark, tall and handsome stranger standing behind her. It was love at first sight!

At the beginning, after Elizabeth had confided to her mother about the escalator incident, her mother was firmly against any possible relationship with a strange Indian man. They met secretly as often as they could, for a few moments exchanging pleasantries on her way home from work. That was not enough for Ali.

He was persistent, grew bolder, and would often ride his bicycle close to her house, hoping to catch sight of her.

One day, Elizabeth's mother saw Ali. She gasped in surprise and said to Elizabeth, "He is so handsome, even I could fall in love with him." From that day on, their courtship was blessed. It was a few months later, during a period when Ali often dropped by for tea and spoke of his plans for the two of them in India, that the two were married quietly in a civil ceremony. She was only seventeen and he, twenty years old.

There was a creaking sound as the door was opened wider, followed by the rustling of the heavy curtains. Elizabeth's spell is broken. She looks up shyly and sees an unfamiliar face of an elderly woman, somewhat austere, dressed in a beautiful purple silk *salwar*. Her slightly greying hair is covered with a chiffon *chunni* of the same colour. Elizabeth is overcome with sudden fear. With her heart beating fast, she bows her head, lifts her arm and greets Ali's mother with a customary *adaab*. At the same time she utters the Urdu words Ali has taught her for this first meeting. "Dadi, you idiot, you fool," Elizabeth exclaims the words in Urdu.

Understandably, Dadi looks shocked. Then it dawns upon her that her son must have taught this young English girl these words. Dadi begins to laugh. Knowing her son and his sense of humour, she understands that this is his way of helping his mother accept this foreigner. Laughing, sharing her laughter with other women who have entered the room to catch a glimpse of this white woman, Dadi draws her up in her arms and clasps her warmly.

While the servants knew of Elizabeth presence in the servants' quarters, they also loved Ali and, at his request, would not betray Ali's confidence to other members of the household, not even to Ali's mother. Dadi was not prepared to have a white woman as her daughter-in-law; in fact, Ali had done nothing to prepare her for this, when he proposed to his mother that she meet a friend of his from London. Ali's possible marriage to this woman would be unheard of in a strict Shia Muslim family where *purdah* was still the custom. Besides, her wonderful son had been engaged, according to custom, to be married to his cousin since he was a child. Now, in this richly decorated room with the portrait of Ali's late father looking down on them, sitting on the rug was this beautiful blonde British woman, her head covered with a *chunn*i, wearing a *salwar-kameez*, waiting for her soon to be mother-in-law to say something.

Dadi, as Elizabeth would come to realize, is a wise woman. She says nothing. Just keeps smiling, then nods her head several times, as if accepting the inevitable.

Before long, Ali's mother and family celebrate their Muslim wedding. Even though their house held touches of an elegant earlier era, the wedding was a simple affair, not ostentatious at all. Some of the family's closest relatives and friends were invited, and they came with gifts of money and flowers. The *Nikka* ceremony is simple. Ali proposes to Elizabeth and they repeat the word "*Qabul*" – "I accept" – three times. Then the couple and two witnesses sign the contract and the marriage is legal! Ali's mother accepts Elizabeth as her daughter-in-law and declares, "From now on, you will be called Zarina." Finally, Zarina can live with her beloved.

Easier said than done. There are so many things she needs to find out how to do. Except for Ali who does she ask? No one speaks her language.

Of course, Zarina's first challenge – one she came face to face with the day she arrived in Hyderabad – was to learn how to use the toilet. Never had she seen anything like this before. The servant girl has shown her the bathroom, but when she entered, all she saw were two cement blocks a foot apart, with a pan on a cement floor, and a tap and a pitcher resembling a tea pot. Where is the toilet paper, where does one sit? Baffled, Zarina had run out of the room. The servant girl took pity on her and quickly showed her how she must squat and wash herself. Zarina is aghast. How will she survive under these conditions? But in the middle of the night, unable to sleep, she makes up her mind. "This is the choice I have made and I must make the best of it," she says to herself.

If she had felt any pangs of separation from her mother and grand-mother, two women now left alone in their small Muswell Hill apartment in London, Zarina had suppressed them well. In the heady excitement of her first days in India, she had all but forgotten them. In her mind, she now started to compose a long letter giving all the details of the wedding, the house, the people around her, and her immense happiness. Eventually, she succeeded in composing the letter, much to the delight of her mother and grand-mother, who couldn't wait for more news from India.

Zarina's next challenge is observing "*purdah*" and living in a joint family. She must stay inside the house and is not allowed to go outdoors. The servants like her and are sympathetic to her predicament. They try to make it easier for her. They use a lot of sign language with her until she slowly starts to pick up Urdu expressions.

Ali's uncle and aunt who live in one wing of the same house are very kind and nice to her. The uncle is a very dignified man – a Moghul who was the state's Chief Engineer and Director of Housing. Her mother-in-law tries to keep her busy with mundane chores like separating *dhal* (lentils) from rice – a meaningless task! But Zarina didn't seem to mind.

Zarina is an intelligent young woman and decides she will learn Urdu so she can converse better with family members and the servants. She also starts to learn cooking in earnest from her mother-in-law. Under Dadi's tutelage, in no time she becomes an excellent cook. Her specialty becomes *korma*, the iconic food symbol of Hyderabadi Muslim household. Family and friends heap praise on her for this absolutely delicious dish Zarina would make with ingredients like coconut, roasted peanuts, roasted onions and served with chicken *dum* biryani. There were other delicacies like the dessert, *fahluda* that were among the first recipes Zarina learned and served to members of her new family. What better way to earn the love and affection of them all?

Once in a while, Zarina accompanies her husband to the Military Club. These outings are rare, and she must always cover her head with a scarf. On occasion, Ali takes her for a drive to see some of the famous historic buildings in Hyderabad. One such building of which Ali was especially proud of was the "*Charminar*".

Just as the marble wonder of the world, the *Taj Mahal*, celebrates the undying love of the Mughal emperor Shahjehan for his beloved wife Mumtaz Mahal, Ali explained that down south in Hyderabad the *Charminar* evokes the eternal romance between Mohammed Quli Qutb Shah and his beloved Bhagmati. Legend describes the young and handsome Quli Qutb Shah as falling deeply in love with the beautiful courtesan Bhagmati. So besotted was he that even the swollen river Musi could not stop him from crossing over to see his beloved. To aid his son, his considerate father, Ibrahim Quli Qutb Shah, ordered a bridge to be built so he could safely meet his lady love. "Such are the echoes of eternal love," said Ali. "If my father had been alive maybe he would've had a bridge built between London and Hyderabad." The bridge became an object of much laughter for Zarina and Ali ever since.

Zarina easily identifies with these feelings of passion and love. For has she not given up all that was familiar to her to come to this strange country far away from home? In spite of what others might think of as sacrifices, Zarina feels immensely content just to be with Ali. There are times she feels slightly amused at the comfortable life and a kind of seedy old world splendour that she had been ushered into.

As the days go by, it is as if Zarina finds her wings. She has to explore every nook and cranny of the city she now calls her home. For an introduction, she was told of the words of a 17th century Qutb Shahi poet who had written, "Hyderabad is the precious stone, the ring of the world. The value of the ring lies in the jewel." Her interest in the monument Charminar led her to legends that suggested there was once an underground tunnel all the way to the mouldering Golconda Fort, a passageway for Kings to escape invaders. Even though she was disappointed the secret tunnel was never found, she was enchanted by the ruined Golconda Fort.

It is said that the 13th century Venetian explorer, Marco Polo, spent many months, perhaps the better part of a year, in India. Except for a brief mention of an inland kingdom that is ruled by a queen and is known for its 'high standard of justice and equity,' and which produces all of the diamonds in the world, his account of India is limited to a coastal belt and ends with this tantalizing remark, 'Of the inland regions I have told you nothing; for the tale will be too long in the telling.' Many believe that the inland kingdom in Marco Polo's diary was Hyderabad.

Before long, the war in Europe has drawn Great Britain into its orbit. Her mother's intermittent letters told her tales of misery and deprivation overcoming English lives. In one of her earlier letters to her mother, Zarina had written excitedly about the famous mountaineers who were on board the ship when she sailed for India. One day, her mother wrote with the sad news that the climbers had come to within eight hundred feet of the K2 summit. In Hyderabad Zarina had read nothing about the expedition, and she cried as she read from her mother's letter that, through a series of mishaps, one of the team members, Dudley Wolfe, was left stranded near the top of the mountain after his companions had descended to base camp. Three attempts were made to rescue Wolfe. On the second attempt three *sherpas* reached him after he had been alone for a week at over 24,000 feet but he refused to try to descend. Two days later the *Sherpas* again tried to rescue him but they were never seen again. A final rescue effort was abandoned when all hope for the four climbers had been lost.

Zarina's mother and grandmother decided to leave London for the Isle of Whyte before German bombs started to pound the city. Elizabeth found some comfort in this, and praised her mother for her spirit of adventure. "I hope you will be happy where you are," Zarina wrote to her mother. "Here is where I'm determined to find peace and happiness. I so look forward to my life with Ali and my child who I'm starting to feel within me."

# Chapter 3

The sound of the truck smashing into the car was loud enough and echoed in the undulating countryside. But there seemed to be no one within earshot. The dust settled down and an eerie silence descended on the scene. Nobody came around, the nearby fields were deserted under the glaring sun. After a while, the truck driver opened the door to his cab and climbed down to the highway. Angry and menacing, he walked purposefully to the scene of the wrecked car and the human debris sprawled within and outside of it. He muttered something at one of the figures on the ground, probably one of the children, and then walked back to his truck.

Within moments, he was away. Silence returned once again.

Several hours later, an office colleague of Ali's drove up to Zarina's house with news of the accident. He had been instructed by the office to fetch Zarina to the hospital. Zarina peppered him with questions but all he could do was apologize and plead no knowledge of the details. The gentleman drove a distraught Zarina through some of the more beautiful sections of the city, full of greenery and far removed from the sand and dust of the desert.

The hospital was still some distance away. Ali had brought Zarina to these same areas and recalled to her stories of Karachi once having had the reputation for its sparkling cleanliness. He had heard stories, Ali said, of Bunder Road being washed clean every night, and of horse-drawn trams with the horses' droppings being swept away as soon as they touched the ground. Also, of *Bakri Id* when goats were slaughtered and someone would stand by with mud and lime powder to repel flies by immediately covering the blood. "Wouldn't it be nice to have a house here?" Zarina had remarked to Ali. Ali had smiled, a smile Zarina was remembering all through the drive to the hospital, and he said, "Yes, someday we will."

While she kept imagining Ali's smiling face, she seemed totally oblivious of her surroundings. In her mind, the desert had crept in and swallowed all the beautiful gardens, homes, and parks she was passing on her way to the hospital. Later, she would admit to Meena that she was not even thinking of her or the children.

"No, no, no! This is not real. It cannot be happening," Zarina cries in anguish. Tears streaming down her face, she sits huddled with Didu and Danny. Little Tayab is back home with the maid. Zarina feels numb, frozen. Through a mist of tears, she sees strange faces around her in what looks like a hospital corridor. There are nurses rushing back and forth. Zarina cannot remember anything. Someone takes her by the hand. She jerks her hand away at the touch. After a moment she looks up and recognizes the gentle face of Ali's cousin Sadiq, a naval officer. Then she remembers the family in Hyderabad had sent a message to him. Luckily, his ship was anchored in Karachi harbour when he received word of the accident involving Ali. "I will help you in whatever way I can", he said.

But Zarina wants answers. "Where have they taken Ali? Where is Meena and when can I see them?" Sadiq tries to explain as gently as he can. "Zarina," he says, "you must be strong. The news I am going to share with you is horrific. I am sorry to tell you that Ali is in a coma. No one is allowed to see him. There is a British doctor who is looking into his case but it does not look good. You must be prepared for the worst. I am so very sorry.

"As for Meena, she is very ill. She has lost a lot of blood but she is alive. Although the doctors at first thought she would not make it, they are willing to spare no effort to save her life. I need you to be strong and agree to what we have to do under these terrible circumstances."

The world is collapsing around Zarina. Suddenly, the beautiful edifice of life with Ali that she had created was beginning to crumble into dust. She tries desperately to summon all her strength and courage. Gradually, she finds herself agreeing with Sadiq. She feels obliged to trust Sadiq to do what he thinks is best.

The next three days are spent in dread, confusion, and tears. They spend most of the hours at the Jinnah hospital, day and night. Zarina does not leave Meena's bedside. She is praying for her and for her beloved, whom she cannot even see. What thoughts go through her mind no one can tell. Finally, on the third day, the doctors tell Sadiq, Ali is no more. According to Muslim rights, the funeral takes place immediately. Tears seem to have dried up within Zarina. She doesn't cry, doesn't wail. Just sits stone-faced, staring into space.

When the funeral is over, Sadiq does not waste any more time. Right away he decides to bring the children and Zarina home to Hyderabad. He is sure that in Hyderabad in the care of good doctors and loving care of the family, Meena will recover soon.

Over the months that Ali and family have been in Karachi, Dadi has passed away. If they had gone back, it would have cost too much money and time for all of them to have travelled to Hyderabad. Besides, by the time they could reach Hyderabad, Dadi would've been buried anyway. But, Ali's Uncle Mirza and Aunty Zainab are there in the house in Hyderabad.

Their farewell to Karachi is unceremonious. Some of Ali colleagues whom Zarina had met on occasions came to share her sorrow and to say how much they will miss her. That was all.

# Chapter 4

Meena, who has not healed well, becomes the centre of attention as soon as they return to the family home in Hyderabad. She has to be hospitalized, and needs much care and attention. Zarina, Aunty Zainab, and Uncle Mirza all take turns staying by her bed. Zarina spends nights in the hospital.

Within weeks, Meena is back from hospital where her condition has improved a lot. But she remains silent and withdrawn, unable to engage in conversation with anyone, not even her mother. Only her sister Didu manages to make a dent on her silence. Zarina often finds them huddled together, whispering. Danny feels alone and left out. He can only find some companionship with the servants' children who become his playmates.

Zarina has always had great affection for the family in Hyderabad, and they for her. She and the children are welcomed back warmly by Ali's uncle and aunt and other family members who drop by to share her grief. This is the home where she had first come to, and there are memories everywhere she turns.

Zarina wants to be happy here but life has changed for her and, although she tries, she cannot forget memories that haunt and torment her. After the Indian army had marched into Hyderabad and Ali lost his position in the army, they both unhesitatingly made up their minds to leave Hyderabad and begin a new life in Pakistan. What made her feel even more helpless now was that, while working with the Transport Department in Karachi, Ali was thinking of getting his papers ready so they could immigrate to England in the future. It was a kind of insurance policy, Ali said, in case things didn't work out for them in Pakistan. But, alas, it was too late. And now she is pregnant with another baby who will never see her father.

As the days pass, Zarina hardens her resolve. She is only twenty-eight. She tells herself, "I will go back to England and make a life for myself and my children. I have my mother there and family. This is what I must do. When the baby comes, if it is a girl, I will call her Zarina." She was constantly reminded of the loving Dadi's invisible presence in every corner of the house, and remembers that this is the name Dadi gave her.

Having made up her mind, Zarina tells Ali's aunt and uncle over dinner one evening, "I must go back to England soon. I cannot burden you with the responsibility of bringing up my children in Ali's absence. Even as I take them to England with me, I will promise all of you I will never convert them to Christianity. They are Muslim by birth and I will respect their father's religion and traditions."

At first, there is total silence around the dinner table. Then tears slowly appear in the eyes of Uncle and Aunt. The family is very sad to have them all leave. After much deliberation, and with great trepidation, the Uncle and Aunt come to Zarina and say, "We have a request which we are afraid you might deny us. But, we know you are kind-hearted and you will feel for our loss. We are asking you to give us your eldest daughter so we can bring her up as our little grand-daughter. We promise you we will take good care of her and cherish her as our own. We propose this as adoption is not allowed in the Muslim religion."

Zarina is totally taken aback. How can she leave behind her eldest daughter? She asks for some time to think things over. Finally, Zarina thinks that the elderly couple have no one. They have been the kindest and most generous family that one could hope for and in her innermost heart she knows that her daughter will be brought up in the midst of luxury, love and will be provided for most generously. If she does not agree, perhaps she will be depriving her daughter of a wonderful future. With these thoughts in mind, she decides to agree.

The day comes for them all to head out to the airport. After all the airline formalities, it is time to say goodbye. Hearts are heavy and there are tears. Suddenly, Meena realizes that her elder sister is not coming with her to London. This cannot be! The two are, and have been, insep-arable. Both cling to each other and no one can tear them apart. The airline is announcing the departure of the plane. There is no more time, but Meena will not let go. Finally, Zarina agrees for the two girls to stay on in Hyderabad. A final embrace and Zarina starts to walk towards the airplane with her boys. The girls stand and watch, waving goodbye to their mother and their brothers. They are crying too, as are the Uncle and Aunt.

# Chapter 5

And so it is that Meena and Didu both go home with Aunt Zainab and Uncle Mirza. But, both girls seem subdued and especially Meena. Although the two girls play together, there are times when the Uncle and Aunt observe them sitting pensive and they appear sad. This especially happens in the evening just before bed. On occasion, they have seen tears brimming over and they are crying. And even worse, Afreen and Hamida the two young women who have become their caretakers, report to Aunty and Uncle that Didu often wakes up screaming in fear. This wakes Meena up and then there are more tears. So, Aunty and Uncle decide they must find out what is at the bottom of these fears. They know that asking them will lead no where, because it seems to them that Didu is unable to talk about what she is afraid of. She has not even spoken to Meena about her fears, and the two are so close to each other.

After a lot of thought, Aunty and Uncle decide to buy the girls a large doll's house. The girls are very excited. They get to furnish it with beautiful doll furniture. Aunty is very good with her sewing machine and together they design and make the curtains and other furnishings. While engaged in this task the girls seem to be feeling better and their spirits pick up. They set up the doll house and introduce into the house characters from their lives. The Uncle and Aunt notice they have their parents, and themselves and Danny and little Tayab. And their play recounts all the things they used to do in their home in Pakistan. Sometimes the Uncle and Aunt play with them and sometimes they like to watch.

One day, while they are watching they observe that Didu is re-enacting the same scene over and over again. It is a very scary scene. They see that scene is that of a car and a lorry accident on a deserted country road. At the scene of the accident Meena is flung out, unconscious on the roadside, Danny is also there hurt but alive. Ali, their father is badly hurt and lies as if dead. Didu then takes a male figure and makes it walk up to the window of the car where she is sitting and, raises a finger and says in a very angry voice "If you ever tell anyone what you have seen, you will not live another day". Her face is pale and she is shaking. It seems that at last Didu is able to let the others know what it is that has been so frightening. Over and over this is the scene that is re-enacted and now Meena, Aunty and Uncle feel they understand what really happened at the accident. At last it is no longer a secret that Didu has been hiding.

Aunty and Uncle gather the two girls in their arms and cover their faces with kisses as they keep telling them that from now on they have nothing to fear. They are safe now and in their protection. Those "bad" people who had threatened them will never be able to harm them.

While reassured, Meena still has questions. She wants to know what happened? Who found her? Where was her father? What happened to him and Tayab? What about Akbar? For months nobody had talked to the girls about the accident. Little wonder that night terrors and nightmares were making it impossible for them. Finally, it seemed that a curtain had been lifted and the circumstances of what really happened that day on the country road in Pakistan came to make sense. That day, late into the night Aunty and Uncle were able to tell them what they knew of the accident. And, Didu was finally able to unburden the dark secret she had been guarding. It was as if the light in the room began to shine brighter and, amazingly, when they looked out the window, a bright moon was shining, filling the room and the doll's house with light.

# Chapter 6

Aunty and Uncle's home was like a warm nest protecting the two girls from the noise outside and the winds of change in Hyderabadi society. Even after India had won her independence, what should have been decades of peace and creativity was marred by violence that erupted like ulcers from time to time. It was not only the tragic battles over Kashmir between India and Pakistan that shook the sub-continent, but even smaller eruptions like the Indian Government's annexations of the Portuguese territory of Goa and the Nizam's fiefdom of Hyderabad. The tremors that sent shock waves from the Hindu-Muslim riots following independence and the death of millions of Muslims and Hindus were followed by the assassination of Gandhi by Hindu fundamentalists in early 1948.

It was at best a tenuous existence even for well off Muslims like Uncle Mirza who read the morning papers and often rose from his chair with a sigh, murmuring, "This does not bode well for us at all."

The girls were happy. They grew quite attached to the two women, Farida and Afreen, whose job it was to look after the two girls. Oftentimes, when they would rather play with their precious dolls' house, Farida would entice them with new games. Sometimes they would dress up in fancy clothes, sometimes they might play with sea shells, and sometimes build a house of cards. In the daytime, their favourite was always 'hide-and-seek'. The house was big and there were endless places and corners to hide in.

Meena loved to tease Afreen, and made it a point to hide whenever it was time for her to have her hair washed. Afreen, whose job it was to wash

Meena's hair and make sure her clothes were well pressed, would often cry out in despair that she was falling behind in her daily chores while trying to find Meena.

She would be calling out for Meena, searching for her in every room, under the beds, moving some light furniture and chests around and humming to herself, "Little Meena loves to play hide-n-seek." Finally, she would beg Meena to come out, which she would do and run into Afreen's outstretched arms.

Didu, on the other hand, is somewhat quieter and does not give Farida, whose duty it is to look after her, any trouble.

Badminton is also one of their favorite sports. Again, Afreen must make deals with Meena. She tells Meena, "We can't play unless you have your hair washed and, of course, you must have your bath." And this is almost a ritual day in and day out once summer has gone and the evenings have become cooler.

In between, there are always a couple of hours when the Urdu, English, and math teachers come to the house and the girls quiten down.

Before the girls can play badminton, Afreen and Farida must get the court ready, sweep it clean of dust. The entire place must be spick and span, for Aunty and Uncle would not want the girls to get sick.

When everything is ready and the badminton net strung up, they bring out two chairs for Uncle and Aunty who watch the games whenever they can. Their applause and encouragement injects a lot of excitement in the games. Aunty is very easy going and never raises her voice. The girls love her to bits. Uncle may look stern, but at the sight of the girls, his handsome face softens.

Tea times often turn into another engrossing ritual. On many an afternoon when they are not otherwise playing with their companions, Meena and Didu just can't wait for the tea service to begin. "Are you going to turn on the samovar?" Meena asks Farida.

"Yes, yes. Do you want to pick which samovar we should use?"

Each samovar consists of a body, a base and chimney cover and steam vent, handles, tap and key, crown and ring, chimney extension, cap, drip bowl and teapot. The body is shaped like an urn. And the teapot is filled with tea concentrate.

Meena thinks for a moment. "Can we have the silver one today?" she asks.

"Of course, you may," replies Aunty. "Afreen do take out the brass plate with all the sweets. The girls must be hungry and there's still a few hours left before dinner."

While they enjoy their afternoon tea, Aunty and Uncle often tell them stories of Hyderabad. These stories fill their imagination with a sense of wonder, and usually precedes visits by the girls to such sights as the Salar Jung Museum, at one time regarded as the largest one-man collection of objects in the world. It was such a large, cluttered museum that it needed visit after visit to see even portions of it.

Following a lesson in the history of the famed musical clock at the museum, one day the girls finally get to see it. Visit after visit, they simply had to see the clock, with crowds of visitors waiting every hour to see the ornamental time-keepers pop out of the clock and sound the gong.

As they grew older, Meena and Didu began to sense the magnitude of the collection. Their impressions would stay with them forever. The clock was only one artifact collected by Mir Yousef Ali Khan, a fanatical collector who had gathered 46,000 objects of art, 58,000 books and 8,300 manuscripts. His prized collections included sculptures, paintings, carvings, textiles, ceramics, metal wares, carpets, arms and armor, walking sticks and other artifacts. There was even a set of ivory chairs presented by Louis XVI of France to Tipu Sultan of Mysore. But what fired Meena and Didu's imagination the most was the dressing table once belonging to the French Queen, Marie Antoinette. They would prod their tutors on information about the French Revolution, about the naïve queen suggesting that her subjects eat cake in the face of starvation, and of course her tragic beheading. Whatever the tutors had to say was augmented in later years by books that they devoured with curiosity, fascination, and horror. Given the stories of the Nawab of Hyderabad's lavish life style, his jewels, wives, Rolls Royce collection, and his gardens, they would breathe sighs of relief that the Nawab's family escaped a fate similar to that of Marie Antoinette.

Museum visits aside, Meena and Didu's life was one of daily routine, occasionally interrupted by a quick round of badminton in the lawn, or simple strolls to see how the flowers and plants were doing. Like other evenings, it would soon be time for dinner.

Farida and Afreen get busy preparing dinner. Aunty likes warm hand-made *rotis*. They light the *enghetti*, a small coal burner. The family sits while Farida and Afreen prepare two brass trays of food. Each tray has one chicken dish, one vegetable dish, one salad and *rotis*. One tray is for Meena's family and the other for their cousin who lives next door.

Dinner is usually a quiet affair. Nobody speaks much. Occasionally, Afreen drops by to ask if anyone would like seconds. The helpings are so large to begin with, nobody asks for seconds.

But weekends are different. As Aunty and Uncle want to introduce them to their British heritage, they have employed a special cook, Lazarus, who prepares English cuisine on weekends. While the girls do not seem too keen to eat this food, they do love the desserts prepared by Lazarus. Meena loves Crème Brulee, and Didu loves Jello and Custard.

Weekends also become special as they go on outings. Accompanying them always is Muniram who, in his liveried outfit, looks somewhat daunting. Of course, Uncle and Aunt are also always with them too.

There are also occasional surprises after dinner. "Afreen," Aunty calls out one evening. "Let me know when the jeweller is here." Tonight, Aunty wants the jeweller to set the diamonds she has picked out recently into a necklace. Meena and Didu are excited. They love to see the shining jewels and feel the hard clear stones. They look at the patterns and help Aunty to choose one.

It is late. The sky is dark and only a few stars are out, shining like the diamonds the girls have just chosen. Their eyes are heavy with sleep and no sooner do they rest their heads on the pillow, they are off to the land of dreams.

Aunty and Uncle lie awake in bed and wonder how Didu and Meena are sleeping. Are they restless, still haunted by memories of the accident? They know the answer. Even now, from time to time, Aunty has to rush to the girls' bedroom in the middle of the night, to find them clutching one another, sobbing. She comforts them as best she can and, sometimes, sing them songs so they can return to sleep. One song she sang often started aptly with the words, *So ja, Rajkumari, so ja* (Go to sleep, my princess, sleep). She would sing beautifully, and continue singing softly until she was certain both girls were fast asleep. Some nights, even the magic of the doll's house doesn't seem to work.

Uncle and aunt never tire of thinking how the girls might some day put the demons to rest. They would give them all the love and affection they could muster, especially because their mother was far away in England. They are totally unselfish and unfailing in this regard. And the girls will grow up happy and curious and loving, that is the elderly couple's dream. They dream of the two getting married, raising children, multiplying joy and happiness. They dream that the girls will discover a new world where divisions have disappeared, where all religions are equally sacred, where there are bridges between communities and nations and people of different colours.

Then a day comes when Uncle realizes that Meena and Didu are more precious than if they were his own daughters. On this particular day, they have a visitor. The servant opens the outer gate and the visitor walks into the house. They hear the sound of his voice and know it is Uncle's friend, Dr. Reddy. Dr. Reddy is the chief engineer and he visits them often. Unfortunately, he has lost his wife a few years ago, and his grandchildren are grown up. He is a lonely man. He insists on dressing as elegantly as he must have done in his youth, visiting friends and acquaintances in colorful Jodhpuri clothes. He is immensely fond of Meena. The first question he asks of Uncle and Aunty every time he visits is, "Where is Meena? Seeing her makes me happy."

On this particular evening he chooses to broach a surprising and awkward subject. "Mirzaji, Zainab Bibi," he begins, "I have a request. Please give Meena to me. I will bring her up as my own grand daughter. What is more, as a token of my gratitude to you both, I will offer you the equivalence of her weight in gold."

At first, Uncle and Aunty were startled, almost stunned. When Dr. Reddy's request had sunk in, their jaws dropped in surprise. In a way they were both deeply touched, but even without a word Uncle and Aunt realized it was impossible. They sat in silence.

Dr. Reddy, perhaps taking heart at this silence, said, "Mirza Bhai, it will be beautiful, a great bridge, a great symbol, for our two communities, our two religions. And the gold could be so much more than her future dowry which you won't have to worry about."

Finally, Uncle found his voice. "Reddiji," he begins, "We are overcome with happiness and gratitude at your most generous offer. But Meena is ours. She is part of our lives, the breath that keeps us alive in these troubled times." He paused and remained quiet and thoughtful for a long time, nodding his head. Then he continued, "Reddiji, you've been a constant friend to us, and we value our friendship more than anything. But this is one bridge we would prefer not to cross." Then, with folded hands, he says, "Please forgive us, Reddiji. You are welcome to our house to see her as often as you want. But from this day on please do not mention this again. We promise, you will always remain our friend."

# Chapter 7

Summer often comes to our part of the world with a vengeance. The cruel heat isn't sufficient punishment, heavy rains and floods often make matters worse. City streets are flooded, stranding cars, spreading fear, misery and filth. From the surrounding fields, snakes rise from their pits and swim and writhe in muddy waters. But life moves on, with all its beauty, ugliness, cruelty against a patchwork of compassion emerging from unknown sources. It was on a summer like this that Meena and Didu's lives were about to take another turn on the road.

As if summer wasn't trying enough, these were troubling times for people in Hyderabad.

Against the backdrop of a long-simmering movement for local autonomy which was born of a Communist-led peasant revolt in Hyderabad's Telengana district a year before Indian independence in 1947, there were demands now to carve out the Nizam's Hyderabad state on the basis of languages. It was like carving flesh, and blood was certain to flow. Sometimes there were heated discussions on this turmoil between Uncle and occasional visitors. The two sisters remained untouched, and Aunty made sure Didu and Meena were not within earshot when arguments erupted.

Didu and Meena have navigated adolescence in the safety and affection of their home, go through their schooling under the watchful eyes of Aunty and soon they reach the threshold of womanhood. Two beautiful women, shielded from an uncertain world.

A time comes when Meena and Didu will be separated. It seems now is the time. As it often happens, Aunty and Uncle are approached by an acquaintance offering his nephew's hand in marriage to Didu. In the absence of their mother, they have jealously guarded the two women as if Didu and Meena were their own daughters. They realize the time has come for them to at least think of parting with one or both the women.

Far from rushing into a decision, Uncle and Aunty leave no stone unturned in making enquiries not only about the proposed groom but also his extended family, most of whom were living in Hyderabad. It takes nearly four months for them to gather all the information and make up their minds. Finally, they consent to the marriage.

Didu and Meena are heart-broken. Where they had spent a childhood clinging to one another in times of sadness and fear, they now find themselves crying on each other's shoulders as they contemplate their imminent separation.

Didu's Muslim wedding is a grand affair. Uncle and Aunty want to make sure that the wedding would be the talk of the city. They did not want either Didu or Meena to feel that their father was not alive to give them the appropriate wedding. The invitation cards are carefully selected and designed on the best paper. Friends and relatives from far and wide have been invited and no expense is spared from making this a memorable affair. The wedding venue is decorated with beautiful garlands of white jasmine and red and yellow roses. Lights have been strung up between the tall trees in the lawn, which is wrapped around with a tasseled *shamiyana*, adorned with lights. The plaintive sounds of classical music from sarods and shehnais can be heard from a day in advance of the wedding. The lavish feasts, noise and excitement fill the air. This was to be a wedding befitting a princess. And so it was.

It was well understood by all that Didu would go abroad with her husband shortly after the wedding. But neither Uncle or Aunty, let alone Meena, can truly reconcile themselves to this eventuality. They are all grief-stricken. Didu is torn between leaving her sister behind in Hyderabad and a rising expectancy over seeing her mother once again after many years.

# Chapter 8

What's this?

The last time we left Meena, she and her sister Didu, whose real name was Safia, were little girls who had suddenly grown into beautiful women living with their Aunty and Uncle in a spacious house. Didu is now gone, to live with her husband in England. Much has happened since that time. Meena has occupied the empty space left behind by her sister's departure with reading and with family stories recounted by her beloved Aunty. There is a growing awareness in her that there's also a beautiful world outside of the house in Hyderabad that awaits her. She feels strongly that there is much to look forward to beyond occasional annoyances and daily hardships, however inconsequential in their case.

It has been over two decades since Meena last spent time with her mother. During all these years, her mother would send her beautiful frocks made in England and her maternal grandmother would send sweaters she knitted for her Uncle. Whenever she wore the dresses, her friends in school would ask where she got them from. When she told them, "My mother who lives in England sent them to me," her friends would wonder why her mother did not live with them in Hyderabad. But Meena would never go into her story. She kept that hidden. The truth about memories is that they are sometimes woven with threads of pain and violence which are better left undisturbed. But that doesn't mean the memories disappear, as Meena knew all too well.

There was only a fleeting visit from her mother after Meena was married. That was so brief and so awkward that Meena seemed to have almost completely wiped off memories of that visit. For the trip to India, her mother had left her brother and little sister, Zarina, with her mother in London. What Meena remembers is how very nervous her mother-in-law was of the 'white woman' coming for a visit. "How am I going to speak to her?" asked her mother-in-law. Meena assured her that all would be well. And, so it was. Surprised, her mother-in-law found that Meena's mother spoke fluent Urdu and enjoyed Hyderabadi cuisine. Her mother had never forgotten the language she learnt as a bride when she first came to Hyderabad. Her mother stayed two months with them that time. That was the last time Meena had seen her mother.

"Has it been that long?" she wonders. Meena is now married to a journalist who works for a prominent newspaper in Hyderabad. She used to see him from time to time as they were neighbors and some years later, after she finished her education, her aunt and uncle arranged for their wedding. They had never dated, never even had tea and refreshments together. The family also lived in Hyderabad, and that's the way it was.

Meena's wedding was also done with as much grandeur as Didu's.

Safia, or Didu as we knew her, now lives in England in Telford, close to where her mother lived. Her husband is an eye surgeon there. They are happy.

Life takes strange turns. Once a long time ago, Meena's father tried to leave Pakistan to come to England because he felt the family would not be safe in Pakistan. And now, Meena's husband faces threats from the political atmosphere in which he finds himself.

The Nizam's Hyderabad which went through communal convulsions when it became part of the Indian Union in 1948 is in turmoil again, thanks to the decades-long simmering political discontent known as the Telangana Movement. This movement, and similar outcries in different parts of the country, were now culminating in the division of Indian States along linguistic lines, historically always a recipe for disaster. Agitation intensified and there were violent protests, police firings and people were killed.

As often happens during periods of political turmoil, journalists were targeted. It was too much for Hyder and Meena.

Fortunately, Meena had a sister-in-law living in Canada. Saddened as she was with what was happening in Hyderabad, she offered to work on their immigration process so they could come and live in Canada. Another bridge was opening up before Meena's eyes, this time spanning the oceans.

After months of waiting, sometimes in anxiety, sometimes in resignation, their immigration papers finally came through. They make up their minds to go.

It is now 1974. As Meena, her husband Hyder, and her two sons prepare to leave India, Uncle and Aunty, however supportive of the move, fearful of the loneliness awaiting them, plunge into despair.

Meena and Hyder try to console them with impossible promises of frequent return visits to Hyderabad, but they all know it is not going to happen. There is nothing the ageing uncle and aunt can do to reverse the inevitable. Not that they would have wished to, their affection for Meena was such.

On the way to Canada they are making a stop in London. Meena and her family are going to meet her mother, her two brothers and the sister she has never seen. This is the sister her mother named Zarina – the name Ali's mother had given Elizabeth when she married Ali. And Safia is also coming from Telford to meet them.

"Is this really going to happen?" Meena asks herself as often as she puts the question to her husband. She can hardly contain herself. Her excitement knows no bounds. She thinks it is nothing short of a miracle that after more than two decades, she is going to meet her mother. Years later, while she can recall her excitement, she finds it impossible to fathom what her true feelings really were then. Yes, she did have many questions stirring in her mind. What will they look like? Will they like her? Will they kiss and hug each other? Will they have anything to talk about? Where will they begin and what will they choose to remember and share? Will her mother recognize her? Meena has often imagined what her mother probably looked like. It seems that in the absence of any photographs being exchanged in the mail Meena had all but forgotten her mother's face from the last time she visited her after her marriage. Will she look like Meena had imagined her to be? To think of it, they really don't know each other at all!

And yet, after the passage of so many years, Meena still remembers the face of her father from the fateful car trip to school in Karachi which ended so tragically.

# Chapter 9

Too overwhelmed to describe what happened next, all Meena remembers is standing in a circle with all her siblings and her mother and hugging each other. They cling to each other as if no one could ever part them again. Tears stream down their faces but they do not move, holding each other, sobbing in each others' arms.

There they are: Didu, the sister Meena had grown up with in their Aunty and Uncle's house, Danny her older brother, and Tab, the younger brother. These were the two boys her mother had left India with. And now there was also her youngest sister, Zarina.

"How handsome my brothers are and how beautiful my sisters." Meena is bursting with emotion. She remembers thinking, "These are my siblings and this is my family. How amazing that suddenly we are all together now!" She wanted to pinch herself to believe that all this was really happening.

Although they had not seen each other since 1951 and it is now 1974, Meena recalls her time with Didu and feels as if they had never been apart. What was it in their blood that made them feel so much a part of each other, bridging the span of years and the space of continents apart? Meena begins to feel she not only knows her mother and each of her siblings, now she can almost read their every thought.

After things calm down a bit, Meena tells them, "I would like to join mother, and take my sons Goldy and Sheroo to spend a week with all of you on the Isle of Whyte, which is now home for mother." Hearing this, Meena's husband, never one to refuse Meena anything she wants, agrees readily. It is planned and settled. They will go to the Isle of Whyte and spend a week there.

Meena and Hyder, weary after their travels, decide to leave London sightseeing for a future visit. Goldy and Sheroo are a little disappointed at first, but this wears off as their grandmother, whom they call Nani, tells them of some of the places they are going to visit on the Isle of Whyte. After spending a couple of days in London, during which Meena's husband goes to visit with his cousins and give the family time to be alone, Safia had to return to London to be with her husband. The siblings are separated once again.

But why the Isle of Whyte? The simple answer is that, for many years after Elizabeth left Hyderabad, she had lived in London, in East End and then in Muswell Hill. There she was close to where her mother lived. But after her mother died, she moved to the Isle of Whyte, because her brother and sister had settled there. The brother, Meena's maternal uncle, was a manager in a bank. Once there, Elizabeth went to work for the Hovercraft Company on the Isle of Whyte.

The Isle of Whyte, situated in the English Channel, boasts of resorts and holiday destinations from the time of Queen Victoria. It is well known for its mild climate, coastal scenery and verdant landscape of rolling fields and pines. The island has been home to Tennyson, Swinburne and Queen Victoria who built her summer residence there. So now on this visit, Meena's mother brings her family back with her to spend a week on the Isle of Whyte. To Meena the place is paradise.

Here in this quiet, peaceful island, Meena and her family have the good fortune to spend more time alone with each other. Situated midst big tall trees, with the ocean in front and a beautiful English garden of roses, primroses and periwinkle, the house is like a doll's house. Never have they seen anything like it. Her mother explains that it is called a mobile home, like the house was put together somewhere else and then transported to this location.

From the moment they arrive, they are busy exploring the garden, walking to the ocean front and finally coming inside to look around the house. Where will they sleep? It's a question the boys want to pose for their grandmother. There seems to be only the living room and one other room. They are puzzled. They think maybe they will be sleeping in the living room in sleeping bags! They are too busy talking and looking around and, before they know it, finally it gets dark. The children are sleepy. The boys cannot help but ask where they might go to sleep.

No problem! Like magic, their Nani takes off a set of cushions from the kitchen chairs. She then pulls down the kitchen table, adjusting the legs and, lo and behold, here was the bed! Sheroo and Goldy, Meena's boys are are very excited and jump on the bed right away. They are no longer sleepy. Meena pulls the drapes aside so they can look up to gaze through the windows at the trees, the thatched roofs of the houses around and the stars twinkling like precious jewels in the sky. They compare notes and decide the stars are no match for some of the the jewels they had seen in the Nawab of Hyderabad's collection. Finally, sleep overcomes them and they enter their own world of dreams.

# Chapter 10

It is early morning and the sun is streaming in. Both Sheroo and Goldy are too excited to sleep any longer. They are up and ready for the day. "What are we going to do today, Nani? "they ask.

Elizabeth is prepared. She knows that these boys need to be occupied. So she has already planned a picnic out for the day to Carisbrooke Castle. While Meena and her husband get the food organized and pack the picnic basket, Elizabeth gets the boys to finish their breakfast of oatmeal and juice. It's a change from the breakfasts the children were used to back in Aunty's house, but they enjoy it just the same.

Elizabeth tells them, "We are going on a picnic and then to see a castle."

"A castle, Nani?" they ask incredulously. "What is this castle called? Do Kings and Queens live in this place? Please tell us more about this place."

Meena and Hyder watch with pleasure as the children now have taken over and want Nani to tell them all about Carisbrooke Castle. Elizabeth tells her grand children, "This is a castle where there are a lot of things to see. It was built a very long time ago and was at one time the place where a certain British King called Charles I lived. Wouldn't you like to go and see it and learn a little about the history of the castle?"

"We would love to see it too, Nani," says Hyder, as the boys seem thoughtful. Turning to his sons, he asks, "You boys remember Golconda Fort back home, don't you? This is something similar."

"Yes, but there was nothing much in Golconda Fort, "answers Goldy, without too much enthusiasm. "All I remember is that if someone clapped at the fortress gate, you could hear the sound way way up inside the fort. What is this castle called?"

"Carisbrooke Castle."

Everything is planned. Elizabeth is organized and meticulous. Meena, Hyder and the children pile into the car and with Nani driving, off they drive to Carisbrooke Castle.

When they are close to their destination, they can see the walls of the castle on the hill top. Nani explains, "This castle was built as a protection against the invading Viking Kings. We will soon climb the steps and go inside and find out what there is to see."

Goldy and Sheroo enter the castle and first want to see the Museum. They are enthralled to see the coat of arms, the artifacts like the King's bed, his night cap, the jewels and other memorabilia. They also see what was considered the oldest Chamber Organ in Britain. There is also a collection of antique vintage children's toys like dolls and board games, but these don't seem to interest the boys much.

Nani then spreads out the map of the castle and right away they want to see something marked as the Donkey Wheel. So they walk over to see that. They find their way to a little dimly lit room and in the center of this room is the body of a well. There, hundreds of years ago water was drawn up to the castle by an oak wheel. At the present time, no one really needs to use the water but the Donkey Wheel is there for show. One of the museum staff members demonstrates how a donkey would work only six to seven minutes turning the wheel and soon a bucket full of water would appear out of the well. Afterwards, for the rest of the day, the donkey would join its friends on the grassy pastures.

What else is there to see? Elizabeth thinks that they might like to see the beautiful chapel which is now a war memorial. Off they walk over to see this. Rather than talk about wars, Elizabeth wants to introduce them to a little bit of British history.

She tells them that not all of British history is cheerful. The boys keep asking her for stories. Wandering through the castle rooms and halls, some that were dark, the children ask, "Nani, do ghosts live here now?"

Nani hesitates but then decides to tell them. "Yes, indeed. Legend has it that there are ghosts that haunt the castle rooms and gardens. People have reported hearing children play in the garden, and a sad dark presence in the room where Princess Elizabeth, King Charles's daughter, died when she was only fourteen."

The boys are quiet and thoughtful but curious. "Will we see any?" one of them asks. Elizabeth laughs and tells them they might be surprised if they are lucky. They continue to explore the gardens and after a while are tired and hungry. Meena and Hyder suggest it is time to make good of the picnic they have brought along. They pick a lovely spot under a tree with a view from the hill top and spread out their feast. As they finish their picnic and pack up, they can see the setting sun. It is time to go home.

What an interesting day it has been. Tomorrow is another day and another adventure on the Isle of Whyte. Elizabeth promises them a visit to Osborne House, maybe a few days later, which Princess Beatrice, the daughter of Queen Victoria and Prince Albert, used as her residence, after Queen Victoria had passed away.

## Chapter 11

The bright sunlight once again wakes both Goldy and Sheroo. After the previous day's adventure, they are all still tired and decide that for the next few days they would rather stay closer to home and perhaps only explore what is in the neighborhood. They remembered seeing from the car a sign which said "Homemade ice cream". They wanted to go and explore what flavours were to be found there. "Nani, can we just stay here today and maybe go to the ice cream store and walk along the beach?"

"We'll make sure you boys get to the ice cream and the beach," promises their Nani.

Of course, there are lots of beaches on this island, but Nani thinks the children have never seen the wonder of colored sands on a beach. After all, most beaches only have golden sand. But here on the Isle of Whyte, she wanted to show them a strange and rare sight – the colored sands of Alum Beach.

Getting there would in itself be an adventure. Nani tells them," Boys, today we are going to take a bus. But it is no ordinary bus."

"How is that? "asks Sheroo.

"Well, we call it an open top bus," explained Elizabeth.

"An open top bus?" they cried. "Does that mean there is no roof?" asked Goldy.

Just then, the double-decker tour bus arrived at the shelter where they were waiting. The boys couldn't wait to jump on. Next question from them – "How long will this trip last?"

"Twenty minutes," the bus driver answered, as the boys scrambled up the steps to the upper level.

Meena remembers being told by her mother that Alum Bay is one of the most picturesque beaches on the Isle of Whyte. The beach is notable for the iconic chalk stacks known as the Needles. As the bus approached their destination, they could see the pristine beach and the chalk stacks spaced in a line disappearing into the sea.

What are those tall white structures called, the boys wonder? "The Needles," Nani tells them excitedly.

As soon as the bus stops, Goldy and Sheroo jump off the bus and run onto the beach. They can't believe what they see. The Needles are interesting enough, but the sand is even more so. The sand under their feet, unlike any other they have seen before, is of many colours. What makes them of different colours, they ask?

Nani tries to explain, using words and terms like 'oxidized' and 'compound' that are written on posters on the wall. But after a while she gives up, observing the glazed look in the boys' eyes.

"Can we take some sand back with us?" they ask. Nani is well prepared for this and from her big beach bag she takes out a couple of glass vials for the children to fill with the sand. She tells them that the shop on the beach has ornaments using the colored sands and sand painting was a popular craft and in Victorian times; it was known as 'Marmotinto'.

After the boys fill the vials and walk over to the shop to see the ornaments and sand paintings, they are finally eager to go for a swim. The water is crystal clear and tempting. Meena takes out their swimming trunks and sends them over to the change area. In no time, they are back, ready to move on, debating between themselves whether to go walk along the beach or paddle and swim in the clear blue water.

The older folk don't seem too keen about swimming, once they've tested the water with their toes. Instead, they spread out the towels and sit on the sand to watch while the children run across the beach and jump into the surf! The sun is warm and to Meena it's heavenly just to sit and breathe in the fresh cool air.

The breeze tastes of salt. It is so peaceful. One can only hear the sound of sea gulls and the gentle surf lapping softly on the sand. Lying on her towel, Meena closes her eyes and drifts away, until she wakes up with a jolt and shudders as the memory of her father's car accident creeps stealthily into her thoughts and awakens her.

Time passes and after a couple of hours, during which the children have enjoyed building sand castles and splashing in the surf, it is time to pack up and catch the bus back. Today, there is no time to take a cruise around Alum Bay. They will save that for the next time they are on this wonderful island. The homemade ice cream too will have to wait.

## Chapter 12

The days are flying past and it will soon be time to leave. But, as promised, there are still a couple of places that Nani wants to show the children. First, she wants to take them to see Blackgang Chine.

"Nani, Nani, what is a Chine?" they ask.

Nani explains that in the Isle of Whyte there are steep-sided coastal gorges with eroding cliffs of sandstone through which the rivers flow to the sea. Many years ago, few people would visit the area now called Blackgang Chine. And slowly Blackgang Chine became a very special place.

The boys are curious, and want to know more. But when Elizabeth tells them, "We are going to a park," their faces reflect real disappointment. They don't seem too excited. Elizabeth elaborates, "It is no ordinary park. It's a theme park.

Blackgang Chine is the oldest amusement park in all of England."

"Grandma, what is an amusement park?" they ask. Having lived in India, the children have never heard of an amusement park!

"Let's go to the park and you will find out what it is," answers Elizabeth.

So off they go to explore Blackgang Chine. Even Nani is surprised when she sees the spectacular location on the steep coastal ravine. She suggests they find a map of the place and then explore the sights. The first site that draws them all is the Skeleton of the Whale. It is truly immense, and it seems Goldy knows all about whales. He tells them, "They are the largest mammals that live in the oceans. You can make them out by their dorsal fins and smooth bodies.

And, they breathe through their blow holes." They are both excited and spend some time examining the skeleton and trying to imagine what it would look like, flesh, blood and bones all melded together.

On to see the next attraction which, the map says, is in Cowboy Town. As the name suggests there is much there about Cowboys. They are both very excited having heard much about cowboys and Indians. They find the saddles, cowboy hats, boots and spurs, the firing caps and guns, all fascinating, never having seen the objects in such close proximity. As usual, these explorations make them hungry and Grandma decides to give them a treat. She takes them all to the Chime Café where they can choose from a menu of burgers, chips, pizzas, hot dogs and of course, ice cream.

Lunch over, they now feel inspired to tackle some of the rides. What is an amusement park without rides? Of course, they must experience some of them. They have memories of ferris wheels and carousels from occasional fairs back home. But they've never seen anything so modern and gleaming. Those rides are here too. They choose the roller coaster, something which they have never experienced before.

Boy, oh boy! This makes their stomachs turn as they go screaming up and down at break-neck speed. They jump out elated, but decide to try something less wild. Perhaps one more ride; they choose the gentle slide. This is much better and they don't have to hang on to their stomachs.

And now it is time to see the animated clock tower. They are so excited because Grandma has told them it is a very special clock. "What is so special about a clock," they ask. They soon find out. As they wait patiently in front of the clock tower, every fifteen and thirty minutes the door of the tower opens and various monsters and goblins emerge from behind the doors. Upon the hour, a troll-like creature lifts the roof up and two giant gargoyles appear next to the clock, rocking back and forth. Sheroo and Goldy are thrilled, beside themselves with excitement and pleasure. They throw their arms around their Nani and give her big bear hugs. Hyder and Meena watch, happy that the visit has turned out so well for the boys. And so the day ends.

# Chapter 13

Nani has saved the best for the last day. This is their last outing on the Isle of Whyte and tomorrow they must start back for London and from there fly to Calgary to start their new life in Canada.

Spring had come and almost gone with a torrent of colours as they drove past the grass meadows leading to Osborne House. Wild daffodils were still springing up all along the valley. Towering trees with thick canopies of fresh leaves stood over the meticulously groomed lawns. Before entering the house one could see more ordered plantings of daffodils and some white and red rhododendrons coming into flower. The predominant color on the west side of the house was generally green, from the grassy lawns.

Osborne House stirred different emotions in different members of this group of visitors. The boys, Sheroo and Goldy, noting the architecture and the orange-yellow walls, immediately started to compare the mansion with the Nizam's palace back in Hyderabad. "This is a museum too," Nani told them, "and it might even remind you of the Salar Jung Museum."

"Certainly less cluttered than the Salar Jung Museum," says Meena, as they enter the building. They grow silent as they move along the corridors with the occasional guards, some smiling, others stone-faced, as they pass. The older members of the group become aware of the confluence of two great societies over which Queen Victoria ruled. Hyder, well honed on societal undercurrents as a journalist, remarked, "I think it's more a bridge than a confluence. In a confluence two forces merge into one and the sum is greater than the individual part. That's not happening here."

Although the matter was not discussed further at the time, the bridge was probably the better analogy – two sovereign nations joined by a history of occupation, independence, and all that has gone back and forth between India and England. This became all too evident as they were transfixed by a long corridor, the walls flanked by large portraits of Indian Maharajahs like the stately Maharajah Duleep Singh and smaller portraits of others. Among portraits of women were the beautiful Maharani of Cooch Behar. There was an intriguing portrait of a young Princess Gouramma, daughter of the deposed Rajah of Coorg. Gouramma has in her hand a Bible, signifying her conversion to Christianity, and her Christian name was Victoria, honouring Queen Victoria who was also her godmother. The portrait of the young and beautiful Kashmiri village girl, Miran, wide-eyed in surprise, evoked gasps of amazement. But it was the portrait of Abdul Karim, by the Austrian artist Rudolf Swovoda commissioned by Victoria to do Indian portraits, that proved electrifying to the visitors.

The story of the handsome Abdul Karim, one of two Indians selected to become servants to the Queen on the occasion of Victoria's Golden Jubilee in 1887, is a story in itself. Victoria gave him the title of 'Munshi' (adviser) and learnt Urdu from him. He was envied and disliked by others in the Queen's family and household, and no sooner had Victoria passed away in 1901 than her successor Edward VII sent him packing back to India and ordered the confiscation and destruction of the Munshi's letters to and from Victoria.

Over the years, people have wondered whether Victoria was in love with Abdul who arrived in her palace four years after the death of her close companion, John Brown, or whether she was fond of him almost as a son. While the young boys admired the sketches of Indian soldiers serving the Empire, the others wondered how genuine Victoria's love for India was, considering she never visited the Jewel in her Crown. Did she look upon her Indian subjects, like many others, as exotic barbarians who needed her rule to come closer to the civilized West? And yet, she took pains to learn Urdu and Hindi and was close not only to Abdul Karim but also to Duleep Singh, the deposed Maharaja of Punjab. And she sent the artist Swovoda to India to draw portraits of her subjects. Perhaps a bridge across the oceans existed in Victoria's mind, even though she never crossed it to visit India.

Their next stop, the Durbar Room, also had a curious history. The refurbishing of this great hall was undertaken by none other than John Lockwood Kipling, father of Rudyard Kipling, who brought to the task an Indian assistant, Bhai Ram Sing. The architectural touches and the Indian motifs proliferate. It is said that Abdul Karim pointed out to Victoria that, as Empress of India, she definitely needed a Durbar Hall.

Whether the story is apocryphal or not, the hall is truly magnificent, worthy of an Empress. A much-needed banquet hall, it was designed for imperial hospitality to impress and intimidate at the highest level. The boys unhesitatingly compared it to the Nizam's banquet room.

On their way out, Elizabeth wants to walk back to the corridor with the Indian paintings one more time. Meena follows her while the others move along. She stops in front of Abdul Karim's portrait, staring thoughtfully at it. Meena moved close her mother and held her hand. Her mother had visited Osborne House before, and yet she confessed being always drawn by the image. Could it be that she shared something common with Abdul's life? That both had had to finally cross the bridge, although in opposite directions. Her mother was back in England, while Abdul spent his final days in Agra.

Like the Mughal Emperor Shahjehan, held captive by his son, spending his final days in Agra Fort, gazing across the river at the Taj Mahal, his wife's resting place, could it be that Abdul's imagination gazed across the ocean to Osborne House, and even Buckingham Palace, from where he had been banished by Victoria's son?

## Chapter 14

The Prairies, the Rocky Mountain, cowboys, cattle ranches. All of these had painted a very romantic image of the Canadian West in the minds of Meena's family, especially the children who had already seen a few cowboys and Indians movies back in India. Bollywood was far from their minds as they were growing up.

Imagine the children's disappointment when told, upon arriving in Calgary in summer, that they had just missed the Calgary Stampede by a few weeks. Would they be able to see the Royal Canadian Mounted Police, upright on their shining horses, going after bad guys? The Mounties, don't they always get their man? The boys would have to wait for the Stampede's chuck wagon races, steer wrestling, and the bull riding.

With no immediate family in Western Canada, Meena and her husband began the slow task of creating a new life for themselves, brick by brick, relationship by relationship, gathering material necessities to run a household. Somewhat away from the tension and nervousness that seemed an unrelenting part of their lives before Canada, Meena and Hyder took to facing their immediate challenges with optimism and energy. Still, Meena's fears persisted, hidden dangers held her a prisoner.

When Meena and her family arrived in Canada in the summer of 1974, there was a lot of political excitement in the air. The Liberal Party having just won a majority government, Canada offered the charismatic Pierre Trudeau his third term as Prime Minister. The new winds of political change hardly touched Meena, who had had enough negotiating political headwinds during her young life. But Hyder, a seasoned journalist, found himself right in his elements.

Having steeped themselves in all the publicity material made available to them by the immigration office, Hyder had reasoned that the city of Calgary probably offered more opportunities to newcomers than older cities like Montreal or Toronto. He was absolutely right.

In August 1974, Calgary was more a large town than a city of any consequence. But with its proximity to vast energy reserves in the province, it had become home to over three hundred oil and gas companies. By all accounts, its economy was growing by leaps and bounds.

For Hyder, there is no suitable opening in the newspaper industry. But his determination and instinct for unraveling problems – honed in his newspaper experience – eventually lands him a job in an insurance company. Over time, Hyder will prosper in his chosen industry.

They found themselves a car and were soon venturing out of their rented apartment to explore different parts of the city. Mostly short trips, in the interest of time and expense. They had decided to make their home in Calgary, and they gradually began to fall in love with the city and whatever charms it had to offer. Hyder's colleagues at work encouraged him to find a more suitable rental closer to his work. Soon, Meena and the children engaged themselves in searching for a place in an area recommended to Hyder – the southwest quadrant of the growing city.

On one of their explorations, Meena spots a little bungalow with sloping grounds covered with summer blooms of poppies and daisies. She falls in love with the place and they decide to move to their new home. The school is not far away, and this was quite a relief. Having to do everything by themselves, they soon realize how exhausting the experience of setting up a house can be for immigrants from countries where domestic help is readily available. They lamented the fact that there was no one to even brew a single cup of tea for them. Thankfully, Meena took on these tasks, her beautiful smile never leaving her face.

Together they had to learn where to shop, how to use the appliances in the house. The family, accustomed to the celebrated cuisine of Hyderabad, made known, without complaining, their taste for the kind of food that demanded meticulous cooking and exotic spices totally unfamiliar to Calgary's supermarkets and grocery stores in the 1970's. There was one, a single Indian restaurant in the southern part of the city and its smaller branch in the north.

It was not until they had become familiar with the local mosque and the Imam that they started making new friends. Their faith and prayers helped give them courage. With their friends' help, small mysteries like where to find Indian spices began to be solved. Calgary had, again, one single grocery store run by an East Indian family where one could find all the cooking spices one needed.

Their new friends and acquaintances also guided them to the importance of attending open houses in their school, to gather information on what to expect from the children's school and what the school expected of them. It was all far more structured than anything they had encountered earlier.

The days pass by as they adjust to their life in Calgary. Hyder has his colleagues at work, and Meena a small circle of acquaintances. The children begin to build friendships more quickly. They are of course in regular contact with Hyder's sister in Toronto. Just a phone call away, she is always ready to give sound advice and guidance. They also exchange many messages with Meena's mother in the Isle of Whyte, and also her sister Zarina. The boys love to talk with their Grandma and go over the exciting adventures during their visit to the Isle of Whyte.

For Meena, it is soon to be an emotional time. It is the time of Ramadan. The time, every year in the ninth lunar month, when Muslims around the world fast, pray, reflect, and bond with their community. For forty days now, Meena and her family will abstain from food and drink from before sunrise to after sunset.

Like other Muslims, Meena is steadfast in her belief that these rituals instill patience and self control. She also believes fasting helps grow compassion for the less fortunate, encourages a focus on spirituality and diminishes the lure of materialism.

Ramadan is a time of renewal, but it also commemorates important sacred events. For Meena it is the time when she lost her father some twenty-four years ago. Not a day goes by when she does not think of her father. She grieves for him over the gulf of years that separate. What would it have been like if he had been a part of her life? Just to be hugged, held and loved by him? It is as if her father's presence died when he died. Nobody in the family talked about him, especially her mother. Perhaps his untimely death was too painful for her.

Now in Calgary, Meena has everything she could want. Her married life with her husband and two sons is blessed. But despite all the happiness, she says there are times when she feels fearful and nervous. She says, "I think we all have something quiet and sad in our hearts. It never leaves us." What happened one fateful day in 1950 is burned in her heart. She cannot shake off the fear that something bad lies just around the corner. Something terrible might happen anytime.

Her thoughts often wander back to the childhood days she spent with her sister Safia, or Didu, in Aunty and Uncle's rambling house. Of a sudden, the dark corners of the house become bright, brimming with memories. Often, when she is resting in the afternoon, she finds herself dreaming of her life with Didu. When she shakes herself awake, she knows they are dreams and nothing else. Because she and Didu were inseparable, sometimes she is startled out of her dreams to believe they might be real. In her family, she can recall several stories of people feeling the presence of loved ones who may be thousands of miles away in a distant land.

Meena knows her sister Didu had recently returned to Hyderabad with her husband. More recently she had news of Didu being ill and facing surgery. Meena has been worried, her afternoon siestas have become fitful and disturbed. On one such afternoon, Meena falls asleep. She suddenly feels Didu's arms around her, embracing her, whispering, "Don't worry. I am happy."

Tears streaming from her eyes, Meena sits up, awakened, longing for the love and warmth of the embrace she felt in her dream. But the dream was over. She spent the early evening hours pacing restlessly, waiting for Hyder to come home from work. She must find out if her Didu is all right. But deep down in her heart she feels as if Didu was paying her a visit to say she was no more. A final embrace to say good-bye.

An equally concerned Hyder places a long distance call to India, and their worst fears are confirmed. Didu has passed away during heart surgery that very day.

# Chapter 15

It is still summer, and the days are long. Gradually, they begin to take in more and more of the city, its centres of higher learning and entertainment venues. But it is getting cooler, and snow can't be far behind.

Calgary had grown from a Mounted Police camp in 1876. When the boys discovered there was a place called Fort Calgary at the original site of the Mounties' camp, they could not wait to pester Meena and Hyder to drive there. But the visit was somewhat anticlimactic, for Fort Calgary was a far cry from some of the forts the boys had seen, like Hyderabad's Golconda Fort or even the more recent Carisbrooke Castle they had seen in the Isle of Whyte.

The children forgot their disappointment when they walked over to a beautiful spot close to Fort Calgary where two rivers met – the Bow river and the Elbow river, very imaginatively named. It was the history surrounding the rivers' confluence that captivated them most of all.

Since nearly eight thousand years ago, Canada's indigenous people had been using the confluence as a place to cross the rivers and set up tents on the dry river bed before the snow melt flooded the place. There was a legend associated with the meeting place of the two rivers that was part of the Blackfoot Indians' lore. How Napi (the Old Man) mapped out the land with pastures, animals, and then made woman and child with clay from the riverbed.

While Fort Calgary was unfamiliar to most of their acquaintances, just about everyone they met asked if they had visited Banff. Meena got tired of saying 'no' every time. Indeed, Meena is never one for long car rides to see anything. A few months into their stay in Calgary, an inspired

Hyder comes home one evening and says, "Did you know, Meena, that the town of Banff is very close. Just a two-hour drive, I'm told. There are also two beautiful lakes nearby, their colours truly spectacular." Then, turning to the boys, Hyder declares, "I believe that on the highway one can sometimes see, if one is lucky, black and brown bears, even Grizzly bears."

That was enough to set the boys off. They could hardly wait to go. There was no turning back. On a glorious Saturday morning, they pack lunch, throw in their jackets, take some extra blankets and pile into the car. The journey starts off with a heated discussion. The boys had done their own research in conversations with friends. They filled lots of small stones in four Pepsi cans and planned to rattle them should bears come too close. Once in the car, much time was spent debating whether one should curl up and play dead if surprised by a black bear, or climb a tree if attacked by a brown bear. There was considerable confusion on which escape strategy worked for which species of bears. "Try both strategies, see which one works," Hyder finally said to end the discussion.

By now, they were on the highway heading west to the Rockies. Suddenly, everyone was silent. The first encounter with the prairies is always something of a spiritual experience for many, an awakening of sorts. The unending stretches of the earth, flat, undulating, sometimes with some distant cattle visible as dark specks, rolls of neatly tied hay lying on the pastures like rolls of newsprint waiting to be transformed into newspapers. But time seems to stand still on the prairies. There is no news, except perhaps for ranchers and farmers, most of whose news is woven inextricably into the seasons, the rain, the snow, the hail, the draught.

The silence inside the car humming along the highway was reflective of highways of the mind which the prairies gently lead adult minds to, if not the minds of young children. The highway curves past the Bow River and other streams as the foothills of the Rockies rise from the edge of the horizon. This was something they had never seen before. Soon the outlines of the foothills give way to the mountains. This too was a new experience, quite different from the hills of Deccan or the Isle of Whyte, still fresh in their memories.

The boys are in the back and Meena up in front with Hyder driving. After about an hour or more, they pass a sleepy nondescript township called Canmore. The place didn't look very welcoming, so they decided to give it a pass. Soon they are at the National Park toll gate after which they stop by the roadside to stretch their legs and get a breath of fresh air.

The children are starting to get hungry, but Dad is the principal decision maker on this debut trip to the mountains, and he decides lunch will be at Lake Louise. The children decide to quell their hunger with some candies while Meena, who has hardly spoken on this trip, stares outside the car window, as if mesmerized by the endless cliffs and swaths of evergreens lower down the slopes.

They drive up to the parking lot at Lake Louise, lunch bags slung across in backpacks. The first stunning view of the lake, cradled as it were in the lap of mountains on three sides, takes everyone's breath away. Lunch takes a back seat for a while as Meena and Hyder sit on the bench and silently contemplate the still waters, its colour a spectacular turquoise. The children run along the lake shore close to the bench, returning excitedly to say they had seen signs saying 'Beware of Bears'. They sit down beside their parents and scan the lakeshore left and right to see if they spot any bears. Not today.

The boys eat their sandwiches without taking their eyes off the lakeshore. Maybe they'll sight bears another time. Before walking back to the car the children ask if it's possible to take a peek inside the imposing hotel by the lakeside named Chateaux Lake Louise. They approach the hotel entrance with some hesitation and ask the tall, liveried concierge if it's okay to see inside. The concierge smiles warmly and ushers them into the lobby. "Take your time," he tells them. It is warm inside, and they spend most of the time staring out of a large window looking directly onto the lake.

They found it difficult to imagine that less than a hundred years ago this magnificent hotel was probably no more than a log cabin. The lake was discovered by explorers only in 1882, but had been known for ages to the Stoney Indian tribe who called the lake 'The Lake of Little Fishes', until the Canadian Government decided to rename it after one of Queen Victoria's daughters.

Before walking back to the car, Meena suggests they take another short walk along the lake-shore. The lake has so captured her imagination she feels sorry to have to go. Meena wonders if Queen Victoria would have preferred Lake Louise to Osborne House on the Isle of Whyte, then laughs aloud at the childish thought.

It is getting late in the day, and both Meena and Hyder begin to get somewhat anxious about returning home. They find it impossible to skip the alpine town of Banff on the way back. The boys were hungry again, and the parents did not want a revolt on their hands. They stop on Main Street in the center of town where every-one watches fudge being made inside a 'fudg-ery'. They taste the samples of course, but each one gets to choose a small packet to take home. Banff's other attractions like the Sulphur Pool and the Banff Springs Hotel are overshadowed on this occasion by the attractions of a pizzeria and an ice cream store.

It is now dark, and time to go home. In the car, the animated discussions of their unique experiences of the day soon give way to a quiet stillness as the boys fall asleep in the backseat, and Meena and Hyder wrap themselves in their thoughts. It has been a long day. There is a tape deck playing soft music but that too ends and becomes silent.

The highway is virtually empty but for an occasional car. Suddenly, Hyder swerves the car and screeches to a halt. Everyone wakes up with a start. Meena becomes strangely distraught.

Hyder suspects he might have dozed off. Thankfully, it is not a crash, even though he stopped pretty close to the guard rails along the highway. He awkwardly asks if everyone is all right.

The boys call out they're fine, but inside the darkened car Meena seems to be sobbing quietly. Suddenly, everyone wants to know what happened to her. But Meena can't tell them. All through the rest of the journey, she keeps the flood of surging memories bottled in her heart. From time to time, Hyder keeps asking if she is feeling unwell, if he should stop. Meena waves with her hand to ask him to keep going.

Once inside their home, and the children gone to bed, Meena breaks down in her husband's arms, unable to keep her thoughts to herself any longer. She sobs and asks why her father had to die in the car accident in Pakistan and who was the stranger who walked over to her sister Safia and warned her never to speak to anyone about the accident. Hyder wipes away her tears and sits her down on the bed. He then opens one of drawers in his desk and brings out a yellowing sheet of paper. A piece of archives he had secured through his contacts in journalism back in India. Hyder is privy to something he has not shared with Meena all these years. It is a news item from the Karachi newspaper 'Dawn' carrying the events of her father's death in a car accident. But is was no accident. It was murder. And the newspaper quoted from the driver of the lorry which smashed into the car and confessed, "I was paid to do it."

Finally, Meena learns that her father was targeted by his enemies at his workplace who had then hired a killer to run him down. Meena doesn't seem to care any more if justice was ever done. Her family remains unaware if any investigations were carried out by the police at the time, or any time later. She is content to have found some peace with the news which her well-meaning husband had decided to shield her from for years.

It is a new day. Meena feels as if dawn is lighting up the heavens and urging her to find solace in the words of the Persian poet, Rumi (1207-1273):

*"Don't be sad because God sends hope in the most desperate moment*

*Don't forget the heaviest rains come out of the darkest clouds."*

THE END